APR 3 0 2007

P9-BIP-351

Dear Parent:
Your child's love of reading starts here!

Every child learns to read in a different way and at his or her own speed. Some go back and forth between reading levels and read favorite books again and again. Others read through each level in order. You can help your young reader improve and become more confident by encouraging his or her own interests and abilities. From books your child reads with you to the first books he or she reads alone, there are I Can Read Books for every stage of reading:

SHARED READING
Basic language, word repetition, and whimsical illustrations, ideal for sharing with your emergent reader

BEGINNING READING
Short sentences, familiar words, and simple concepts for children eager to read on their own

READING WITH HELP
Engaging stories, longer sentences, and language play for developing readers

READING ALONE
Complex plots, challenging vocabulary, and high-interest topics for the independent reader

ADVANCED READING
Short paragraphs, chapters, and exciting themes for the perfect bridge to chapter books

I Can Read Books have introduced children to the joy of reading since 1957. Featuring award-winning authors and illustrators and a fabulous cast of beloved characters, I Can Read Books set the standard for beginning readers.

A lifetime of discovery begins with the magical words "I Can Read!"

Visit www.icanread.com for information
on enriching your child's reading experience.

For all the children and all their dreams
—B.B.

For BB,
whose creativity, compassion, and strength
are ever an inspiration
—G.K.

HarperCollins®, ♣®, and I Can Read Book® are trademarks of HarperCollins Publishers

Library of Congress Cataloging-in-Publication Data
Bottner, Barbara.
Pish and Posh wish for fairy wings / by Barbara Bottner and Gerald Kruglik ; pictures by Barbara Bottner.—1st ed.
    p. cm.—(An I can read book)
    Summary: Best friends and beginner fairies Pish and Posh receive encouragement from the Monster Under the Bed as they each try to make wise wishes in order to earn their wings.
    ISBN-10: 0-06-051419-1 (trade bdg.)—ISBN-10: 0-06-051420-5 (lib. bdg.)
    ISBN-13: 978-0-06-051419-8 (trade bdg.)—ISBN-13: 978-0-06-051420-4 (lib. bdg.)
    [1. Fairies—Fiction. 2. Monsters—Fiction. 3. Wishes—Fiction. 4. Magic—Fiction.] I. Kruglik, Gerald. II. Title. III. Series.
PZ7.B6586Pis 2004
[E]—dc22
2005022862

1 2 3 4 5 6 7 8 9 10 ❖   First Edition

I Can Read!

READING 2 WITH HELP

Pish and Posh

Wish for Fairy Wings

By Barbara Bottner
and Gerald Kruglik

Pictures by Barbara Bottner

KATHERINE TEGEN BOOKS
An Imprint of HarperCollinsPublishers

Posh poured the juice.

She didn't spill it.

She put cereal in a bowl.

She didn't drop any flakes.

She made raisin toast for Pish,

her very best friend.

"Good morning. Here's breakfast!"

said Posh, happy with herself.

"I smell something burning!"
said Pish.

"Why do you always burn the toast?"

"Everything but the toast is perfect!"
said Posh.

"You are not careful," said Pish,
who liked things to be just right.
"How can you be a good fairy
if you don't get things right?"

"We need to be careful
so we earn our wings!" said Pish.
"*The Fairy Handbook* says
we each have four chances
to make a wise wish.
Then we get our fairy wings."
"I want fairy wings most of all,"
said Posh.

"Fairies who burn the toast
don't get wings.
They are too *slapdash*," said Pish.
"I am not slapdash!" cried Posh.
She ran into the bedroom
and threw herself on the bed.

"*Ouch*. Please, no bouncing,"
said a voice from under the bed.
"But I am angry!" said Posh.

"I would be angry too
if somebody called me *slapdash*
and didn't like my breakfast
because of one burnt piece of toast,"
said the voice.

Someone understood!
Someone took her side.
"Whoever you are," said Posh,
"I love you!"

"I am the Monster Under the Bed."

Posh peeked underneath the bed.

A pair of eyes stared back.

"Hello, sir," said Posh,

a little afraid.

"Hello, Posh. You can call me Mub.

This is your bed,

and I am your Monster," said Mub.

Pish walked into the room.

"Who are *you*?" she asked

when she saw Mub.

"I am the Monster Under

the Bed," he said.

"I've always been scared

of monsters," said Pish.

"But you don't seem scary."

"I'm not scary," said Mub.

"By the way, are you missing

this blue puzzle piece?"

"I was! Thank you," said Pish.

"My pleasure," said Mub.

He put it where it belonged.

Pish and Mub began a new puzzle.

When they finished the frame,
Pish said, "Excuse me, Mub,
but we must start
our wishes now.

The Fairy Handbook

says we must wish wisely

to get our fairy wings."

"And then we'll learn to fly!"

said Posh.

Posh opened *The Fairy Handbook*.

She began to mark the pages.

"What are you doing?" called Pish.

"I am underlining

the important things!" said Posh.

"Please do not write in the book!"

said Pish.

But Posh underlined anyway.

"You don't listen to a word I say!

If you listened,

you would not lose things,

or burn toast."

"I wish you would listen to me!"

Pish yelled.

"I don't think you're going to like

that wish," said Mub.

The wish worked!

It worked *too* well.

Now Posh erased all the lines.

She found Pish's lost book

about roses and the top

of the puzzle box.

She made perfect toast.

Pish liked this new Posh.

A little later Pish said,

"Let's read a story!"

"Too much to do," said Posh,

who was finishing her chores.

Pish noticed Posh

wasn't humming.

She didn't skip and she didn't fuss.

Pish didn't like this new Posh
after all.

"Posh, you're not POSH-like anymore!" Pish said.

"I'm the Posh you wished for," said Posh.

"I miss the Posh who asked to read a story when it was time to clean up," said Pish.

Making the right wish

was not easy, Pish thought.

"I wish, I wish, I wish Posh
would return!" shouted Pish.
Now everywhere Pish looked,
there were Poshes.
Poshes in the hammock,
Poshes nibbling cookies
and singing silly songs.
"Posh!" called Pish.

The Poshes stopped.

"Yes?" they all said together.

Which was the real Posh?

"I want the real Posh back!"
Pish hurled herself on Posh's bed.
"Uh! My *head*," groaned
the Monster Under the Bed.
"Oh, Mub," said Pish.

"*I wish everything was the way
it used to be.*"

When Pish looked outside,

she saw Posh on her hammock.

"Posh! Is that really you?"
Pish asked.

"Of course," said Posh.

"Everything is fine then!"
said Pish.

"Not really," said Mub.

"You have only one fairy wish left.
And you are no closer
to your fairy wings."

"If Posh was not so slapdash,"
said Pish, "I wouldn't have
wasted three wishes!"

"You wasted your wishes?"
asked Posh. "*That* is slapdash!"

"Friends! Friends!" said Mub.
"Arguing is not the way
to become fairies who can fly."
"Who asked *you*?" said Pish.
"I wish you would disappear!"
And Mub was gone!

"That was a horrible wish," said Posh.

"I got angry," said Pish.

"Now," said Posh,

"it's my turn to wish!"

"I wish Mub would return,"
said Posh.

"That is the first good wish
I have heard all day!"

"Mub, is that you?" Posh cried.

She looked under the bed.

There was nobody there.

"Only his voice is back,"
Pish told her.

Magic wishes
were tricky for Posh, too.

"Pish, remember how Mub

helped you with your puzzles?"

asked Posh.

"And remember how he understood me?"

"I remember," said Pish.

"And he said we shouldn't argue."

"Let's learn how to get Mub back,"

said Posh.

"But you can't be too bossy.

And don't read so fast

that I get confused," said Posh.

Pish and Posh opened

The Fairy Handbook

and sat down to learn

magic together.

"Let's not argue," said Pish.

"Fairies don't argue" said Posh.

"I know that!" said Pish.

"You always know

everything," said Posh.

"It's true," said Pish.

"And I also know how to be good."

So Pish was good.

"Where do I start?" Posh asked Pish.

Pish didn't say,

"Begin at the beginning!"

Instead, Pish said,

"At the top of the page."

And when Posh asked,

"What does this word mean?"

Pish didn't say,
"Don't you know that word?"
Instead, she said,
"You are doing fine."

Posh read *The Fairy Handbook*
until the very end, which said,
"Now you know how
to wish wisely."
Posh wished wisely.

The Monster Under the Bed

was under the bed again!

And Posh had glittery fairy wings!

Pish needed wings too.

"I wish," said Posh, *"for sparkly*
fairy wings for Pish
so one day we both can fly."

There was a loud noise.

Posh and Mub went to find Pish.

All by herself,

Pish had made Posh's bed higher

for Mub.

"I love my new Under the Bed,"

said Mub.

"But please, no more bouncing."

There *was* bouncing.
Two fairies who make magic wishes
and have their fairy wings
may have as much fun as they like.
It says so on the very last page
of *The Fairy Handbook*.